THE
VOYAGE
OF
MUDJACK

All the best

Dyls Hill.

Douglas Hill

THE
VOYAGE
OF
MUDJACK

Illustrated by

Anthony Lewis

MAMMOTH

For LOREN

with much love and no spiders

First published in Great Britain 1993
by Methuen Children's Books Ltd
Published 1994 by Mammoth
an imprint of Reed International Books Ltd
Michelin House, 81 Fulham Road, London SW3 6RB
and Auckland, Melbourne, Singapore and Toronto

Reprinted 1995 (twice), 1996

Text copyright © 1993 Douglas Hill
Illustrations copyright © 1993 Anthony Lewis

The right of Douglas Hill to be identified
as author of this work has been asserted by him
in accordance with the Copyright, Designs
and Patents Act 1988.

ISBN 0 7497 1722 X

A CIP catalogue record for this title
is available from the British Library

Printed and bound in Great Britain
by Cox & Wyman Ltd, Reading, Berkshire

Contents

1	Dreams	7
2	Halyard	16
3	Pursuit	24
4	Escape	32
5	Falling	41
6	Rumbledeep	49
7	Riverton	56
8	Recovery	64
9	Seafaring	73
10	Orlop	82
11	Heroes	90

Chapter 1

Dreams

Mudjack might never have left home if it hadn't been for the magic boat.

In a long-ago country named Riverland, because it was full of rivers, Mudjack lived on a large river called the Tanglewave. There his parents owned a big, slow ferryboat that carried people and things across the river. And, with Mudjack, they also lived on the ferry. So Mudjack had

spent much of his young life going back and forth across the river. Back and forth, time after time, day after day, endlessly.

Sometimes, though, in between customers, the ferry stood idle for a while. Then Mudjack could climb down from the ferry and play. He often went swimming, for like any river boy he had learned to swim at an early age. Of course he swam safely, near the shore, though he liked to dive underwater to see what lay on the riverbed.

At other times he stayed on land, playing on the river bank – finding shells and stones, chasing frogs and voles. But best of all, he loved digging in the muddy river bank. He dug deep squishy holes, or long squelchy trenches, getting happily covered in mud from top to toe. Which is why most people called him Mudjack rather than just Jack.

But by the time he was eleven, Mudjack was growing a little tired of the river-bank mud, and more interested in what was on the river itself. Instead of digging, he would often just sit quietly and watch all the boats that passed. Boats that were going places, upriver or downriver. Not like the ferry, just going back and forth *across* the river.

Watching those other boats, Mudjack dreamed dreams – of going voyaging, upriver or downriver, to see all the strange and interesting things that would surely be there. Especially, he dreamed of voyaging to the very edge of Riverland, to where all the rivers came to their end, when they reached the sea.

More than anything else, Mudjack wanted to see the sea.

Once, when he had been younger, he had asked his father why they couldn't sail the ferryboat down to the sea. His father had laughed.

'Ferry goes across the river, son,' he had said. 'Not down it.'

Mudjack had scowled. 'When I get big,' he had told his father, 'I'm going to sail away to see the sea.'

'Never mind all that, Jack,' his father had said. 'When you get big, your mother and I will need you *here*, to help us run the ferry.'

From then on Mudjack never again talked about going away. But secretly,

in his heart, he couldn't bear the idea
that for the rest of his life he would go
nowhere except back and forth, back
and forth, across the Tanglewave
River. Never going on a voyage to find
strange and interesting things. Never
seeing the sea.

Sometimes the thought of all that
back-and-forthing settled on his mind
like a crushing weight. At such times

he tried to make himself feel better by getting off the ferry, when it was idle, and wandering as far as he dared along the river bank, watching the boats on the river, dreaming his dreams.

That was what he was doing on the morning when he found the magic boat.

He was watching a beautiful tall yacht sailing past. And his head was so full of dreams that he didn't see the rope. A thin rope, stretched across the river bank, with one end tangled in the branches of a fallen tree that had been washed up on to the shore. Mudjack only noticed the rope when he tripped over it and fell full-length in the mud.

Sitting up, he saw that the rope was tied to a small boat, floating at the water's edge. It was a trim, neat boat, painted green, with odd markings along the sides and large eyes drawn on the bows. It had no oars, but it had a short mast and a tightly furled sail. Most oddly, it had no rudder or anything else to steer it with.

It must have got untied somehow, Mudjack thought, and drifted downstream until its rope got tangled in the tree. Probably its owner would be looking for it. But the river was very long, and the owner could be anywhere. Finders keepers, Mudjack thought.

Not that Mudjack knew much about sailing. You didn't learn things like that on a ferry. When he climbed into the little boat that morning, he wasn't really planning to do anything with it. He was playing. He was pretending that he was going to sail away on a voyage.

He sat down near the stern. 'All right, boat,' he said aloud. 'Let's go see the sea.'

'Fine,' said a voice. 'I've always wanted to see the sea.'

Mudjack spun around, staring at the empty river bank. 'Who's there?' he demanded. 'Who said that?'

'I did,' said the voice, sounding amused – and very close. 'My name is Halyard . . .'

'Where *are* you?' Mudjack interrupted.

'You're sitting in me,' said the voice with a laugh. 'My name is Halyard. I'm a boat who can talk and do a great many things. And if you untie me, I'd be glad to take you to see the sea.'

Chapter 2

Halyard

Mudjack sat very still with his mouth open. 'A t-talking *boat*?' he stammered.

'Right,' said the voice. 'I was made by a magician named Fenmire. And I was made *for* someone who is the worst river pirate in the whole country.'

Mudjack's mouth fell open a little more. He had heard stories about things like magicians and pirates and so on, in Riverland. But he had never expected to find anything like that on his own river bank.

'What . . .' he tried to ask. 'How . . . Why . . .' But all his questions got jumbled and in each other's way. And the magic boat, Halyard, laughed and explained.

He said that the pirate, Captain Bully Bargepole, was a huge man who was as lazy as he was fat. He usually made his pirate crew do all the work, the attacking and robbing of other river boats, while Bargepole himself did almost nothing. But, Halyard said, Bargepole liked to *watch* his men at their evil work. So he had a special, magical boat made for him.

That was Halyard – a boat who could talk, to keep Bargepole company, and who could sail himself, so that all Bargepole had to do was sit lazily back and enjoy himself watching his pirate crew in action.

It was not enjoyable, though, for Halyard. He hated watching all the horrible fighting and robbing and everything. And he disliked the rest of the time, too, when he would be tied up doing nothing at the pirates' secret hideout.

'That's all I've done, all my life,' Halyard said. 'Sailing out to watch the pirates, sailing back to be tied up. Never going anywhere else, anywhere nice or interesting. Just out and back, out and back . . .'

'I know what that's like,' Mudjack said.

By then he was no longer feeling dazed and speechless at having found a magic boat. He was feeling thrilled. And he began to tell Halyard about his own life – about the ferry going back and forth, and his dreams of voyaging, and even how he got his name.

'I think your name suits you, Mudjack,' Halyard said with a laugh. And his eyes looked back at the mud down Mudjack's front, from where he had fallen over the rope.

Mudjack tried to wipe some of the mud away. 'How did you get here, then?' he asked, changing the subject.

'By accident,' Halyard said. 'The magician's spell didn't make me able to untie my own rope – probably so I wouldn't sail off by myself. But a few days ago Bargepole didn't tie me up properly. The knot came loose and I drifted downstream. Then my rope got tangled in this tree, and because I couldn't get loose the tree dragged me along when it washed up here.'

'I'm glad it did, Halyard,' Mudjack said warmly.

'I'm glad too, now,' Halyard said. 'But I was really upset at first. Getting caught like this just when I thought I was free, and on my way to see the sea.'

Mudjack sighed. 'I've *always* wanted to go and see the sea.'

'Me too,' Halyard said. 'Ever since I learned that that's where all the rivers go.'

They were both silent for a moment, thinking about their shared dream.

Then Halyard moved slightly, as if tugging at his rope.

'So,' he said, 'if you'd just get my rope free, Mudjack, we can make a good start during the rest of today.'

'Start?' Mudjack asked.

'Yes,' Halyard said, 'just a start. It'll take a few days, I think, to go *all* the way.'

'All the way?' Mudjack repeated again.

'All the way to the sea,' Halyard said. 'We *are* going, aren't we? Isn't that what you said, at the very first?'

Mudjack gulped. This was no longer a game. It was a real magic boat, ready to carry him off on a real voyage. And he wasn't at all sure about it, really. It would mean leaving his parents, being all alone, perhaps running into danger . . .

'Don't worry, Mudjack,' Halyard said kindly. 'Once we've seen the sea, I'll bring you right back. There's nothing to be afraid of. I'll look after you.'

Mudjack sat up a little straighter.

'I'm not afraid,' he said, as firmly as he could. At least, not very much, he told himself. And of course he wouldn't be all alone, on the voyage. He'd be in a magic boat.

'Are we going, then?' Halyard asked.

'All right,' Mudjack said, trying to keep his voice firm. 'We're going. I . . . I just need to get some things.'

He dashed back to the ferry. His parents were busy on the far side of the deck and didn't notice him as he crept below to their living quarters. There he grabbed his waterproof jacket, in case

of rain. Then he used a small kitchen knife to cut chunks of bread and cheese, which he stuffed in the jacket pockets. As an afterthought, he put the knife in a pocket too.

Finally he wrote a note, to leave behind. 'Dear Mum and Dad,' the note said. 'I am going away for a little while to see the sea. Do not worry, I will be fine. See you soon, love, Jack.'

A few moments later he was leaping into the magic boat again. 'All ready,' he said breathlessly. 'Let's go!'

Halyard laughed. 'You have to get the rope, Mudjack. Remember, I can't untie myself.'

Feeling a bit foolish, Mudjack quickly untangled the rope from the fallen tree. Back in the boat, as the river current drew them away from shore, he watched Halyard's sail rise magically up the mast. And even though the breeze was blowing from in *front* of the boat, they sailed smoothly away.

'Off we go!' said Halyard happily.

'Off we go,' Mudjack echoed. And though he still felt nervous, he also felt more wildly excited than ever before.

hapter 3

Pursuit

Mudjack had hoped to start seeing strange and interesting things almost at once. But, for the first few hours, the Tanglewave River and its banks looked much the same as they had looked near the ferry. In that time Mudjack saw nothing more interesting than some frogs leaping among the floating pads of water lilies.

Even so, he went on feeling excited. He was off on the voyage of his dreams – and, on a big river like the Tanglewave, you could never tell what lay ahead. Every bend of the river held a promise that remarkable things might be waiting, just out of sight.

But Mudjack was also still feeling nervous. Along the way he and Halyard had gone on talking, telling each other more about their lives. Which meant that Halyard had told Mudjack a great deal more about the evil Captain Bargepole and his pirates. Those stories were upsetting enough in themselves. But they also reminded Mudjack of a question that he should have asked at the beginning.

He didn't *want* to ask the question, because it put a cold shadow of dread over his excitement. But he had to know. So, at last, he took a deep breath, and stiffened his spine, and asked, 'Halyard,' his voice was a bit shaky. 'Do you think . . . Is there any chance that the pirates will . . . come after you?'

For a long moment Halyard was silent. 'It's a good question, Mudjack,' he said at last. 'I don't really know. But . . . they might.'

Mudjack shrank down on to his seat, feeling the dread send an icy ripple along his spine.

'Though they'd be taking a big risk, if they did,' Halyard added. 'The river wardens have been trying to catch Bargepole and his men for years.'

Mudjack sat up a little, his spine feeling better.

'All the same,' Halyard went on thoughtfully, 'Bargepole is a terrible *miser*. He hates to lose anything that belongs to him. He'd certainly hate to lose his special magic boat – after he paid Fenmire the magician a heap of gold for me.'

Mudjack shrank down again, shivering.

'Of course,' Halyard continued, 'he's also very lazy. He might just send his pirates after me. And they're really not very bright – not without Bargepole to tell them what to do. They might not even figure out which *way* I went. So . . . we ought to be safe from them.'

After all that, Mudjack didn't know whether to feel better or not. And Halyard glanced back, seeing him looking pale and upset.

'I'm sorry, Mudjack,' Halyard said. 'I didn't think. You must find all this very scary.'

'Well . . .' Mudjack said.

'But I really do think we'll be all right,' Halyard added. 'I'm a *magic* boat, after all.'

'Well . . .' Mudjack said again.

'Tell you what,' Halyard said. 'We'll find a safe place to hide, overnight – and then see how you feel in the morning. If you're still worried then, I promise I'll take you straight home.'

'Well . . .' Mudjack said for the third time. He could see that the late afternoon was growing the longer shadows of twilight. They would never get back to the ferry before dark. And despite all his dread he wasn't completely sure that he *wanted* to go home. Not when Halyard seemed certain that they would be safe.

'All right,' he said. 'But couldn't we keep going, through the night?'

'Not in the dark,' Halyard said. 'We might run into something. Anyway, magic boats need to sleep as much as anyone. So let's look for a place to hide.'

Looking around, Mudjack could see nothing at all like a hiding place. The river banks were still as flat and muddy as ever, with only a thin bush or a small tree here and there. But they kept searching as they sped along, while the sun set and the twilight deepened and the coldness grew and spread along Mudjack's spine.

Before long, though, with the dusk, a welcome evening mist came drifting over the water like a veil. And a short while later, Mudjack glimpsed the spreading shape of a large tree looming at the river's edge. A tall weeping willow, its branches trailing down to the water like thick green curtains.

'Look, Halyard!' he said. 'The tree!'

'Perfect!' Halyard said. 'With the mist as well, no one will see us under there.'

Quickly the boat slid in among the drooping branches. Mudjack tied Halyard's rope to one branch, so they wouldn't drift away while they slept. Then he nibbled some of his bread and cheese, though he felt too nervous to be hungry. He was also sure he would never be able to get to sleep. But when he wrapped himself in his jacket and curled up – and when Halyard magically spread the sail over him like a cosy blanket – he was sound asleep within moments.

Perhaps it was a movement of the boat that woke him. Or a rustle among the willow branches. In any case, in the middle of the night, he woke up, peered out over the edge of the sail – and went still, as if frozen.

Shadowy figures were moving slowly towards the boat, in the darkness of the river bank.

And the figure that was closest was the hugest, fattest man that Mudjack had ever seen.

Chapter 4

Escape

Bargepole, Mudjack thought, trying to keep from shaking with fright as he huddled in the darkness under the sail.

The pirate chief was tall as well as enormously fat, with a greasy tangle of hair and a huge dark beard. His coat was fastened by a leather belt around his huge stomach, with an ugly, broad-bladed sword stuck through the belt. And one of Bargepole's enormous hands rested on the sword, as if he was eager to draw it.

The other pirates, following behind their captain, were also evil-looking and armed. And beside Bargepole stood a skinny bald man with a stringy beard, wearing a tattered robe and holding a short, slim staff covered with weird markings.

'There, Cap'n,' said the skinny man with the staff gleefully. 'I said my magic would find him, and it has.'

'An' you'll be paid, Fenmire,' Bargepole said in a deep, harsh voice. 'Soon as you finish the job. Soon as you put a spell on him so he won't never run off again.'

'Glad to,' said the skinny man, who was Fenmire the magician. 'Maybe bring him closer, to be certain.'

A squat pirate with a scarred face untied Halyard's rope and gave it a tug. And with that, at last, Halyard's eyes flew open.

'Bargepole!' he cried in terror.

'Aye,' growled the pirate chief. 'An' you'll get no chance to run off again, Halyard, when Fenmire's through with you!'

Again the scarred pirate pulled on the rope, while the magician raised his staff.

'Mudjack!' Halyard cried. 'Help!'

The appeal, and the terror in the boat's voice, struck through Mudjack's own fear. Without stopping to think, he sat up from under the sail. Amazed, the pirates peered through the darkness.

'What's this?' Bargepole growled. 'A stowaway? Or maybe a thief, who *stole* my boat? I'll feed you to the fish in pieces, boy!'

As Mudjack went icy with terror, the scarred pirate gave the rope another jerk, and Halyard cried out again. Desperately, Mudjack reached into his jacket pocket for the little knife he had brought, and slashed at Halyard's rope.

The rope gave way just as the scarred pirate pulled at it again. He stumbled back, crashing into Fenmire, both of them toppling over. And Halyard, free, fled at full speed out into mid-river.

Luckily, nothing was in their way as they vanished into the shadowy mist. Mudjack heard Bargepole roaring behind them, and saw a few blazing streaks of light that were probably Fenmire's magic, searching for them. But they sped away unseen, downriver, with the noise of the pirates fading behind them.

'Thanks, Mudjack,' Halyard said at last, sounding as shaky as Mudjack felt. 'I'll never forget what you did. It would have been horrible to be Bargepole's prisoner for ever.'

'Will . . . will . . . they chase us?' Mudjack asked.

'Probably,' Halyard said gloomily. 'Especially with Fenmire's magic to help them. And Bargepole won't stop to think about river wardens, if he's angry enough.'

He certainly seemed *very* angry, Mudjack thought. And he felt the coldness like layers of ice along his spine.

'I'm sorry I put you into danger,'

Halyard said softly. 'I suppose I should take you home now.'

Mudjack thought about that. It didn't seem a good idea, since going home meant going upstream, where the pirates were. While if they kept on downstream, anything might happen. The pirates might give up, or might get caught by the river wardens, or anything.

At the very least, if he and Halyard were very careful and watchful all the time, they might be able to stay ahead of the pirates, and even *report* them to the wardens. And then . . .

Then he and Halyard could go on to see the sea.

'No, Halyard,' he said at last. 'Let's keep going and see what happens. Maybe everything will be all right.'

'That's what I hoped you'd say,' Halyard said, sounding pleased.

So they sailed carefully on through the rest of the night. Nothing got in their way in the darkness, no pursuers came storming along behind them.

Mudjack even managed to doze a little, despite all the terrors. But he was wide awake, trying to put the terrors behind him, when morning arrived on the river.

And the morning, he found, brought some interesting things for him to look at. Lively villages, and farms, and animals in fields, and noisy inns, all began to appear along the riverside. While of course the river itself was still busy with other boats.

Mudjack gazed happily at it all, almost forgetting about the terrors. But not quite – because of the people in the other boats. Many of them behaved oddly, waving and beckoning at Mudjack, and calling out to him. But he never quite heard what they were saying, because Halyard never went too close to them.

'We have to be careful,' Halyard explained. 'Bargepole has spies everywhere, to tell him about boats worth robbing. We don't want them coming after us too.'

So they kept away from other boats, trying to ignore the people who waved and called. Before long, it grew even harder to hear what the people were saying, because of another sound. A deep, soft rumbling, like the growl of some monstrous, faraway beast.

Neither Mudjack nor Halyard had any idea what the sound was. But it seemed that they would soon find out, for as they sailed on the sound grew louder, showing that they were getting closer to it.

Oddly, there were fewer and fewer boats on the river around them, as they went on. And the people on those boats seemed more and more anxious to talk to Mudjack. Then, finally, one boatman brought out a huge megaphone, and shouted through it.

'Get off the river!' he shouted to Mudjack. 'You're heading for the Thunderfroth . . .'

But Mudjack and Halyard had no intention of leaving the river, not when any stranger might be a spy for

Bargepole. Nor did they know what a Thunderfroth might be, though Mudjack thought it sounded quite interesting, and looked forward to seeing it.

'Maybe it's the thing that's making the strange noise we can hear,' Halyard said.

Mudjack nodded. Certainly the noise was even louder, no longer a giant faraway growl, more like a giant nearby roar.

In that moment, they swept around a bend in the river and saw, as well as heard, what lay before them.

'I expect that's the Thunderfroth,' Halyard said calmly.

A waterfall.

Chapter 5

Falling

It was a very good name for a waterfall, Mudjack thought numbly. The roaring had become a monstrous thunder, painful to the ears. And it was terrifyingly clear, too late, what all the people in the boats had been saying.

That the mighty Tanglewave River rushed along to the edge of a great cliff, and fell thunderously over.

And Mudjack and Halyard were about to go over with it.

Of course there were no other boats on the river, so close to the falls. Some people were staring from the shore, but they could do nothing to help. Mudjack could tell that Halyard was fighting to get to the land, but even his magic was helpless against the river's current. The Tanglewave had become a torrent, its unbreakable grip rushing them forward faster and faster.

Ahead, where the torrent fell over

the cliff, the spray flew up in a huge cloud of frothy droplets, lifting and spreading, swirling and dancing, filled with the brightness of rainbows like streams of jewels. It looked stupendously beautiful. Or it would have, if Mudjack and his boat hadn't been about to sail over the edge.

As he made a strangled sound of terror, Halyard glanced back at him. 'Don't be afraid, Mudjack,' Halyard said. 'I've been over waterfalls before. Just take a deep breath, and hold on tight.'

The sail slid magically down from the mast and wrapped protectively around Mudjack. He huddled down, closing his eyes, clutching the sides of the boat in a desperate grip. And if he cried out, his cry was lost in the thunder all around him, as the little boat reached the edge of the falls – and tipped over.

Down and down they fell, straight down along the sheer cliff of falling water. Mudjack's grip was so tight that

his fingers hurt, his ears hurt from the overpowering noise, his chest began to hurt because he couldn't breathe in the heavy, drenching spray. On they fell and on, and Mudjack opened his eyes to see other things falling with them – planks from wrecked boats, broken branches from trees, startled-looking fish. Dimly, in the depths of his terror, he wondered if he would suffocate in the spray even before he struck the water that would be waiting for him below.

Then, in the midst of the thunder, he faintly heard a high-pitched sound that he realized was Halyard's voice. At first he thought that the boat was screaming. But then, amazed despite his terror, he made out the sound more clearly.

'Wheeeeeeee!' Halyard was yelling, as if he was having the most wonderful, exciting ride.

An instant later, Mudjack glimpsed what lay below, at the foot of the falls. An immense, wild expanse of water, a pool as broad as a lake, foaming and thrashing endlessly as all those millions of tons of river water plunged unstoppably down into it.

As Halyard and Mudjack plunged, in the final moment of their fall.

Mudjack squeezed his eyes shut again, still gripping the boat, wishing he had the breath to scream in what he thought was the last moment of his life. So he didn't see Halyard's sharp bow strike the water as neatly as a diver's hands. Nor did he see the dark water close around them as Halyard's dive took them down like a stone into the great pool's depths.

But when they shot upwards again, even more swiftly, Mudjack opened his eyes. And when they rose up and up and finally popped out of the water into blinding sunlight, Mudjack opened his mouth and took an enormous gulp of wonderful air. While Halyard bobbed on the frothing surface of the pool, as lightly as if he was made of foam himself.

Half-drowned, half-stunned, unable to believe that he could still be alive, Mudjack coughed and choked and gasped and took more deep breaths. Whereupon Halyard did another astonishing thing.

He *shook* himself, as a wet animal does. And all the water in the boat was flung away, all the wetness soaking Mudjack and the sail and everything – leaving them not only unharmed but totally, magically dry.

'You . . . it . . . that's . . .' Mudjack babbled, unable to find words for his astonishment.

'Great dive, wasn't it?' Halyard said proudly. 'That's one of my best bits of magic, being able to dive underwater. I think old Fenmire used a better spell to make me than he realized. He'd be surprised at all the things I can do.'

Somehow that struck Mudjack as funny. And when he laughed, Halyard laughed along with him.

'Anyway, Mudjack, you needed a wash,' Halyard added.

Mudjack looked down and saw that the mud on his clothes, from when he had tripped over Halyard's rope, had all been washed away.

'I'd rather not have any more shower-baths like that, thanks all the same,' he said.

And they were both still laughing as they sailed away from beneath the falls.

Chapter 6

Rumbledeep

Their laughter died away when they saw that they were sailing out on to the broadest, hugest river that they had ever seen. It must be more than a mile wide, Mudjack thought, peering at the distant shores.

'This will be the Rumbledeep,' Halyard said. 'I've heard the pirates speak of it – the biggest river in the land. Lots of other rivers flow into it, as the Tanglewave does.'

'Are we close to the sea, then?' Mudjack asked hopefully.

'I don't know,' Halyard said. 'I suppose we must be.'

Mudjack sat back, smiling. I'm really going to see the sea, he thought. And then he bit his lip, glancing back at the rainbow-bright spray of the Thunderfroth towering high behind them.

'Hal,' he said, 'do you think the

pirates will still follow us?'

'Not over the falls,' Halyard said with a laugh. 'Not without a magic boat. But . . .' He paused, thinking. 'There *will* be other ways to get to this river. Ways around the falls, for ordinary boats.'

Mudjack's heart sank. 'Will the pirates know those ways?'

'I expect so,' Halyard said calmly. 'But it may not matter. Bargepole might even think we were wrecked in the waterfall. At the least, it'll take

them a longer while to get around the
falls. By the time they can get to the
Rumbledeep, we'll be *far* ahead. I don't
think they'll catch us.'

That made Mudjack feel better. He
still looked back quite often, but he was
able to start enjoying the voyage again.
And there was plenty to enjoy. The
Rumbledeep was a terribly busy river,
with serious traffic problems. Streams
and fleets of boats swept by, big and
small, fast and slow – dinghies, gigs,
houseboats, longboats, pinnaces,

trawlers, sloops and so many more that Mudjack grew dizzy trying to look at them all.

Still, Halyard moved easily enough on that overcrowded river, keeping in shallower water near one river bank where the traffic was a little less. Smoothly he twisted and veered and dodged this way and that, neatly managing to avoid all the other boats.

After a while, Mudjack realized that another boat was doing just the same thing, close behind them. It was a long, light skiff – full of men pulling powerfully at its oars.

'Halyard,' Mudjack said quietly, 'see that boat behind us? With all the men? I think it's following us.'

Halyard rolled his eyes back for a look. 'I think you're right,' he said. 'Bargepole has ways of sending messages very quickly, so he could have every villain on the river looking for us.'

'And this lot has found us,' Mudjack said.

As he spoke, the men in the skiff saw him staring at them. They grinned nasty grins and pulled furiously at the oars.

'Heave, lads!' one of them yelled. 'Just a little boat an' a little boy – but a *big* reward from Cap'n Bargepole!'

All the men laughed evilly as their skiff hurtled forward.

For an instant Halyard stayed

perfectly still, as if frozen with fear. Mudjack wanted to shout, to urge him on, but he felt frozen himself. The skiff raced towards them, and one man in the bow began reaching out with a long pole that had a hook on the end.

But at the very last second, Halyard moved. Magically he spun around, then zipped away towards the nearby river bank.

The skiff had no way to turn so swiftly. And, because the men had been so intent on Halyard, they hadn't seen what was in front of them. A high-sided keelboat, under full sail.

With a splintering crunch, the keelboat rammed into the skiff. The men were flung into the river, shouting and swearing, while louder yells and curses came from the deck of the keelboat. And while their pursuers thrashed in the water, Halyard and Mudjack dashed away.

As he swerved neatly under the bow of a heavily laden lighter, Halyard had to slow down with other boats in the way. And Mudjack jumped when a voice spoke from above him.

'Smart bit of sailin', that, laddie,' the voice said.

Mudjack looked up nervously, and saw a cheerful red-faced man at the rail of the lighter, puffing on a pipe.

'Smart sailin' is what's needed round here,' the man went on, smiling. 'An' it gets worse, down by the city.'

'City?' Mudjack echoed.

'Capital city,' the man said. 'Riverton. Downriver just a short way — on the sea coast. You'll have to take care, sailin' to Riverton.'

'We . . . I mean, I will,' Mudjack said. ''Bye,' he added, as Halyard slipped away through a gap that had opened up among the boats around them.

'We certainly will have to be careful,' Halyard said sourly, 'if the traffic *does* get even worse at Riverton.'

Mudjack nodded, his eyes bright. 'But did you hear what he said, Hal? The city is just a short way from here — on the *sea coast*!'

Chapter 7

Riverton

On they sailed, through the rest of the day. As twilight arrived, they found a small cove with a pebbly beach where many boats had been pulled up on shore for the night, some of them turned upside down in case of rain. It wasn't hard for Mudjack to pull Halyard on shore as well. Halyard then magically folded his mast flat and turned himself upside down like the others.

Again wrapping himself in the sail, Mudjack slept cosily underneath the little boat that night, feeling quite safe. In the darkness, to any prying eyes, they would have looked no different from any of the other overturned boats.

Next morning, several people came down to the cove to get their boats – but they paid no attention to Mudjack as he and Halyard got themselves back on to the river. Mudjack nibbled at the last crumbs of his bread and cheese for breakfast, while Halyard sailed on downstream, towards the great city of Riverton.

The river became even more enormously wide as they reached the city, so Halyard still stayed close to the bank. There the water's edge was lined with huge docks and wharves and piers, with warehouses and storage places behind them, and cargoes being loaded or unloaded everywhere. Like

any river front, it was a noisy, crowded, cluttered place. But beyond the docks, the city was beautiful.

It stood on several hillsides, sloping gently up from the river. On those slopes Mudjack saw leafy parks, wide sweeping avenues, tall graceful buildings, all in greater numbers than he could have imagined. And on top of the highest hill stood the most glorious sight of all – a splendid palace made of creamy white stone, with bright flags flying from all of its delicate towers and spires.

'The royal palace,' Halyard said.

They both gazed at it for a long moment. Mudjack knew little about Riverland's royal family, except that the king and queen were said to be kindly rulers, and that they had a young daughter, the princess. He had never expected to be that close to royalty, to be actually gazing at the palace.

But he and Halyard quickly found that the water by the city's docks was

no place to stop and stare. The Rumbledeep had been crowded outside the city, but by the docks it was positively swarming, seething, jam-packed. Hundreds, perhaps thousands of boats were inching and nudging along, this way and that. And among them Mudjack noticed several sturdy launches painted blue with gold stripes – the boats of the river wardens, trying to keep order and keep the traffic moving.

Halyard, too, could only creep slowly along in the midst of that traffic. But

Mudjack was in no hurry, enjoying himself as always with such a wealth of interesting things to look at. Until he was startled to hear a great shout go up, from the riverside not too far away.

Mudjack stood up in the boat, trying to see. 'What's happening?' he asked. He was actually speaking to Halyard – but a brawny woman in a rowboat ahead of him thought he was speaking to her. She turned, with a friendly smile.

'They'll be cheering Lily,' she told Mudjack. 'She's arrived at last.'

'Lily?' Mudjack repeated.

'The princess,' said the woman. 'Once a week she comes to the river to go boating, and everybody comes to watch and cheer and all. See, over there, by the royal pier? That shiny little one-master? That's Lily's boat.'

Mudjack looked where she was pointing. He saw a small sailboat, brightly painted in white and gold, standing out from the riverboats around it like a swan among mudhens.

It was tied up to a pier painted in the
same colours and decorated with flags.
And a group of well-dressed people was
walking on the pier, towards the boat –
with, in their midst, a small blonde girl
dressed in blue, wearing a bright crown
on her head.

The brawny woman tugged at her oars. 'I'm going to try to get closer,' she said. 'Take care, laddie.'

As she moved slowly away, Mudjack thought that getting closer was a good idea. But he and Halyard found that everyone else on the river seemed to have had the same idea. In the end, as all the other boats pushed and jostled forward towards the royal pier, Mudjack had to settle for a position near a crumbling old dock some distance downstream. There Halyard had a space of open water around him, while all the other boats were still trying to push forward.

'Sorry, Mudjack,' Halyard said. 'I really don't want to get caught in the middle of that mob.'

'That's all right, Hal,' Mudjack said. 'I don't imagine there's much to see, anyway . . .'

As he spoke he caught a glimpse of the little princess climbing down from the pier into her sailboat. He lost sight of her then – but suddenly a great cry rose all around, not a cheer that time but a cry of shock and dismay.

To Mudjack's surprise, a number of men on the boats nearest the royal pier began pulling off coats and boots and diving into the river. And then he caught another glimpse of the princess, standing in her sailboat, looking terribly upset, her hands clasped and tears running down her cheeks.

And there was no longer a crown on her blonde curls.

The people around the pier were still shouting, and Mudjack heard their words quite clearly. 'The crown!' they were shouting. 'Gone! Fallen in the river! Oh, poor Lily!'

Chapter 8

Recovery

Like everyone else in that huge crowd, Mudjack watched in sympathy as the men kept diving, coming up empty-handed, diving again, while the princess waited and wept in her boat. Looking at her tears, Mudjack very much wanted to do something himself to help her, though he couldn't think what. Not until Halyard looked thoughtfully back at him.

'You know, Mudjack,' he said, 'those men may be diving in the wrong places. The river current could have carried the crown downstream from the royal pier.'

'Downstream?' Mudjack repeated. 'Towards *us*?'

'Exactly,' Halyard said. 'So perhaps I should go down and see if I can spot it.'

'Go *where*?' Mudjack said with disbelief.

'Underwater,' Halyard said.

'Remember the waterfall – I can go underwater easily. And no one's watching. They're all too busy looking at the princess and everything. Come on, Mudjack. Take a deep breath and hold on tight.'

Mudjack did as he was told, trying not to think of what had happened the last time he had to do those things. And Halyard sank beneath the surface of the river without a ripple.

The water seemed dark and murky at the bottom of the river, so that Mudjack could see very little. But Halyard's magical eyes seemed able to see perfectly well. With his bow tipped slightly forward, Halyard moved back and forth across the riverbed in wide sweeps, like a hunting dog.

Within a moment, even before Mudjack started to feel uncomfortable holding his breath, Halyard stopped. Above them was the rusting hull of an old fishing smack, tied up to a wharf. From its deck the tangled remains of an old fishnet straggled down, reaching all the way to the riverbed.

'Look,' said Halyard, seeming to have no difficulty speaking underwater. 'At the bottom of the net. There's something bright, all tangled up.'

Mudjack peered through the murk, and saw something glinting faintly. It could just be an old bottle, he thought. Or . . . it could be a crown. In any case, he realized, the next move was up to him – for Halyard, with all his magic, had no hands to pick the thing up with.

He slid out of the boat, swimming with sure strokes, using the old fishnet to pull himself deeper. When he took hold of the glinting object and pulled it free, it stirred up a blinding cloud of silt and mud from the riverbed. So he hadn't seen the thing clearly by the time he was back with Halyard, both of them rising swiftly to the surface.

As they came up, Mudjack saw that not a single person in the crowd seemed to have noticed their sinking or their return. Everyone was still staring fixedly at the royal sailboat and the unhappy princess. Even when Halyard shook himself as before, flinging away all the water from himself and Mudjack, no one looked their way.

But by then Mudjack no longer cared if they looked or not. He was gazing openmouthed at the object in his hands. A small, decorated circle of gold, studded with jewels.

'The crown,' he whispered.

'They don't call you Mudjack for nothing,' Halyard said merrily. 'You're

really good at swimming underwater.'

Mudjack smiled. 'So are you,' he said. Then his smile widened as he glanced over at the royal pier. 'Now let's go and make the princess happy again.'

As they set off, Mudjack stood up, holding the mast with one hand while proudly lifting up the crown with the

other. At once the people in the nearest
boats noticed, and began to call out.
The news spread in a ripple of sound –
and the people began to move their
boats to make a path, an open watery
corridor through the crowd, so that
Halyard could sail right up to the royal
pier.

By then the princess had gone back up on to the pier from her boat. So Mudjack too climbed on to the pier, with the crown, while all the people in that huge crowd of boats smiled and shouted and waved and cheered their heads off.

Mudjack was quickly surrounded by the people who had come to the pier with the princess – probably servants and things, he thought. And then he was face to face with the princess herself – who smiled and wept at the same time, with happiness, as she took the crown from him and put it on her head.

Then she gave Mudjack a hug, and giggled when he looked embarrassed, and asked him to tell her *exactly* how he had found the crown. And because she was gazing at him with such admiring eyes – and because she was the princess – Mudjack found himself telling her the truth. About himself and Halyard, and his magic, and how they had dived deep to regain what she

had lost.

'A *magic* boat,' the princess marvelled, gazing from the pier at Halyard.

'That's right, Your Highness,' Halyard said brightly.

All her servants gasped to hear the boat speak. But the princess just smiled a sweet smile and looked at Mudjack again.

'I love to go boating,' she said.

Mudjack blinked. 'So do I, Your Highness.'

Her smile grew even sweeter. 'I would love it even more in a *magic* boat,' she said softly. 'So would you take me boating, Mudjack? We could sail wherever we wished, all day long. It would be such fun . . .'

Chapter 9

Seafaring

'Your *Highness*!' One of the servants, a tall narrow woman with a long nose, was looking horrified. 'You *cannot* go off with some strange boy, in some even stranger boat! You have your own lovely sailboat, where *we* can all go *with* you – just as your father the king has ordered!'

The princess glanced at her white-and-gold sailboat and wrinkled her nose. '*You* may take the sailboat,' she told the servants, 'and come along after us. If you can keep up. But *I* intend to go boating with my new friend, who rescued my crown.' She paused, peering at Mudjack. 'That is, if you want to, Mudjack.'

'I . . . yes,' Mudjack said, feeling a little dazed. 'I'd be glad to take you boating, Your Highness.'

She smiled happily. 'Wonderful! But – could I just call you Jack? You don't really seem very muddy . . . And you could stop all that Highness-ing, and call me Lily.'

'Um . . .' Mudjack said, swallowing. 'Whatever you say, Your High . . . Lily.'

'*Princess!*' cried the tall narrow woman, still horrified.

The princess turned her back, ignoring the others. 'Where shall we sail to first? You decide, Jack.'

From somewhere Mudjack found the courage to say what he wanted to say. 'We . . . we could do what Hal and I came here to do. We could go and see the sea.'

'The sea?' Lily said, puzzled. 'But it's just *there*, at the mouth of the river.'

'I know,' Mudjack said. 'But Hal and I have never seen it.'

Lily laughed. 'Then we'll go, Jack! Off to the sea!'

She stepped lightly down from the pier, with Mudjack behind her. And while her servants scrambled to get on to her sailboat, and raise its sail,

Halyard slipped away from the pier and sailed off through all the boats full of cheering people.

Laughing, Lily urged Halyard to more speed as they sailed downriver, glancing back at her own boat that was toiling along far behind. 'Oh, this is fun!' she cried. 'I *never* go anywhere without all those people crowded around me the whole time! *Thank* you, Jack and Hal!'

'Any time, Princess!' Halyard said breezily.

'And *look*!' Lily said. 'There it is!'

Mudjack looked – and there it was.

The enormous mouth of the Rumbledeep River was gaping wider and wider. And beyond it was nothing but an enormity of bright, greenish-blue water, reaching as far as anyone could see, looking as if it might stretch all the rest of the way around the world.

'The sea,' Halyard whispered.

Mudjack could only nod slowly, all speech and nearly all thought driven out by the sheer wonderful vastness spread before him. He breathed deeply of the air's salty tang, he listened with delight to a seabird's shrill cry, he stared out at the misty, faraway horizon with a half-smile on his lips while without his knowing it a tear of pure happiness ran down his cheek.

And the princess understood, and wisely remained quiet, while her two new friends gazed and gazed at the sea in wonderment and awe.

But before long they had had enough of silent gazing. Then they found that the sea was a place not only for awe but for play. Halyard rode the crests of giant rolling waves towards shore, all of them shrieking with joy as the waves foamed beneath them, splashing them with spray. They skimmed at high speed over the water, rushing up and down the great slopes of the waves as if on a roller-coaster ride. They chased seagulls, played tag with a dolphin, followed schools of small bright fish that darted just below the surface.

Until at last their happy time ended. The princess's sailboat came into view, battling over the waves, with all her servants leaning over the rails, waving and calling frantically.

Lily sighed. 'I have to go back,' she said sadly.

'I know,' Mudjack said. 'You don't want to get into trouble with the king.'

'But we could come out again,' she said suddenly. 'If you . . . if you would be my very own boatman, Jack. You and Halyard. We could go boating together all the time, wherever we liked.'

Mudjack stared at her, completely startled. Be a royal boatman? Was it possible? He had dreamed, at first, of nothing more than a voyage to the sea, never sure that it would ever happen, never imagining that so much *else* would happen. Finding a magic boat, going over a waterfall, being chased by pirates, meeting a princess . . .

And now, being offered a new life. Which would be, in a way, as if his voyage would go on and on.

His other choice was simply to go back to the ferry, back to travelling across the river, over and over. And that would be the end of the voyage, the end of all excitement and magic.

He knew then that he didn't want it to end. Despite all the terrors that he had met on the voyage, he knew that he couldn't just turn around and go back to his former life.

'Go on, Mudjack!' Halyard urged him. 'Say yes! It'll be fun! And I'm sure your mum and dad will be pleased!'

Mudjack swallowed, hesitated, then shakily nodded. 'All right. Yes. I'd be glad to be your boatman, Lily.'

'Hurrah!' shouted Halyard, while the princess clapped her hands and gave Mudjack another hug, which didn't embarrass him quite so much as before.

Then they turned back towards the city, whisking past the bow of the royal sailboat. And as all the servants called out, struggling desperately to make the sailboat begin its slow turn, to follow

them, Lily and Mudjack waved at them
cheerily and laughed.

They went on laughing as they sped
upriver towards the royal pier. Much of
the crowd of other vessels had left by
then, but there was still enough traffic
near the city's docks to make Halyard
begin to slow his speed. Until, all at
once, he came to a sudden, shocking
stop – with a huge jolt that sent
Mudjack and Lily tumbling to the
bottom of the boat.

When they got untangled and sat up
to see what had stopped them,
Mudjack's spine went icy cold.

Another boat was in front of them,
blocking their way. Another small
sailboat, painted green, with eyes on
its bow and no rudder. And there were
two men in the boat – one a huge
bearded giant in a dark coat, the other
a skinny bald man in a tattered robe.

Bargepole the pirate and his
magician Fenmire.

And the magician was holding his

slender staff with its weird carvings,
pointing it at Halyard and grinning
nastily.

Chapter 10

Orlop

'Hal!' Mudjack said desperately. '*Run!*'

'Don't try it, Halyard,' Fenmire snarled. 'You can't outrun my powers. I could stop you or sink you in an instant, if I have to.'

Bargepole laughed, a deep ugly

rumble. 'Thought you'd got away, did you, Halyard? Never thought I'd get Fenmire to make me a *new* boat that can do everythin' *you* can do!'

'*Hal!*' Mudjack said.

'Hang on, Mudjack,' Halyard said quietly. 'We're not finished yet.'

Then Lily stood up, glaring at the huge pirate. 'Stop this at once,' she said sharply, 'and get out of the way. I am the royal princess . . .'

But her crown had come off when she and Mudjack had fallen over, and it lay half-hidden in the bottom of the boat. So all the pirate saw was a small girl in a damp and crumpled dress.

'Shut up, girlie,' Bargepole growled. 'I dunno what you're doin' here, but if you're a princess I'm a fairy godmother.' He turned to the magician. 'Right, Fenmire, do what I told you. I got me a *good* boat now – so you can turn Halyard here into stone and let him sink. An' the brats with him. That'll teach 'em to take a boat away from *me*.'

Mudjack opened his mouth to yell for help. But before he could make a sound, an amazing thing happened. Halyard *laughed*.

'You call that a good boat, do you, Bargepole?' he said. 'It looks slow and stupid to me. Does it even have a name?'

'Course I got a name,' the other boat said in a rough, loutish sort of voice. 'I'm Orlop. An' I ain't slow nor stupid neither. Like the cap'n says, I can do anythin' *you* can do. Maybe more.'

Mudjack listened, puzzled and curious as well as frightened. But Bargepole was ignoring the two boats, watching Fenmire as the magician lifted his staff and began to mutter the eerie words of a spell. Which didn't seem to worry Halyard at all.

'Anything I can do?' Halyard said calmly to the other boat. 'Really? Can you sail all by yourself without a passenger?'

'Course I can,' Orlop said. 'Easy.'

'Very well,' Halyard said, still ignoring the magician and the spell that was building, 'can you sail at speed against the wind?'

'Any time,' Orlop said with a sniff. 'Probably faster than you an' all.'

By then Bargepole was starting to frown suspiciously at Halyard, while Fenmire had paused in his spell-making to find out what was going on. But still Halyard ignored them.

'You think so, do you?' he said calmly

to Orlop. 'Well, I'll bet there's *one* thing you can't do. What about *this*?'

Then, very softly, he murmured, 'Mudjack – Lily – *hold tight* !'

And he tipped himself sideways, and turned completely over.

Luckily Mudjack and Lily had done as they were told, without knowing why. So they stayed in the boat, clinging to the sides, as Halyard kept on turning – all the way around, until he came upright again. The princess had even been quick enough, as the boat first began to tip, to snatch up her crown so that it, too, would be safe. Then, again, Halyard shook himself to fling out all the water, leaving himself and his passengers quite dry.

'Here . . .' Bargepole began, his frown deepening.

But Orlop wasn't listening. He was laughing, with a sneer in his voice. 'That?' he said to Halyard. 'Nothin' to it. Watch.'

And he tipped suddenly over, just as Halyard had done.

But Orlop had given no real warning. So when he came upright again, as Halyard had done, his passengers did not.

Bargepole and Fenmire remained in the water, floundering and flailing, splashing and spluttering. Bargepole was roaring foul curses and dire threats, while Fenmire was simply screaming, when he wasn't choking on river water.

'Help!' the magician was screaming. 'I can't swim!'

Watching, Mudjack wondered if he should dive in and help, before the magician drowned. But then Bargepole grabbed on to the side of Orlop, and with his other huge hand dragged the frantic magician over so that he too could cling to the boat.

But that was as far as they could go.

The skinny magician wasn't strong enough to pull himself up over the boat's edge, no matter how wildly he struggled. Also, he had lost his staff, and was in too much of a panic to put together any kind of magic spell.

As for Bargepole, he was far too fat and heavy to get himself into the boat. Every time he tried to hoist himself up, his great weight tipped Orlop over and flung him back into the river.

By then Mudjack and Lily were almost falling into the water themselves, from laughing. And also by then all the noise and wild splashing was attracting attention.

While Bargepole and Fenmire went on noisily failing to get back into their boat, two other boats came over to see what was happening.

Two solidly built launches, painted blue with gold stripes, full of uniformed men. River wardens.

Chapter 11

Heroes

The wardens took a look, then a closer look, and finally also began to laugh.

'I can't believe it,' said one with a sergeant's stripes on his sleeve. 'Captain Bully Bargepole himself, right here in daylight, making a fool of himself for all to see.'

Bellowing, Bargepole tried once more to clamber into his boat. Once more his weight tipped Orlop over – and the short mast came down with a solid *thud* on the pirate's head. Half-stunned, Bargepole fell back, floating like an exhausted whale.

'Pull 'em in, men,' the sergeant said, 'and get irons on 'em. This is the biggest catch we've made for years.'

As the wardens dragged Bargepole and Fenmire into one of the launches, chaining them with heavy manacles, the sergeant frowned at Mudjack. 'And

what've you young 'uns got to do with
this?'

That was when Lily coolly lifted up
her crown and put it on. Which made
the sergeant go wide-eyed, and stiffly
salute.

'Beg pardon, Y'r Highness,' he sputtered. 'Didn't know it was you.'

Lily pointed at Bargepole. 'That man stopped us, Sergeant, and was threatening us.'

'He won't be threatening anyone again for a long time, Highness,' the sergeant said grimly. 'And with their leader out of action, we should be rounding up the rest of his pirates very soon.'

He saluted again as the blue-and-gold launches pulled away with their captives. And Mudjack and Lily smiled at each other with relief and gladness.

'What an exciting time I've had!' Lily said. 'And, Halyard, you were *wonderful*, the way you defeated those two!'

'Brilliant!' Mudjack agreed.

'Thought it was a rotten trick, myself,' grumbled a loutish voice.

Surprised, Mudjack and his friends turned to see Orlop – whom they had nearly forgotten – floating next to them.

'Orlop, they were going to turn me to stone and *sink* me,' Halyard pointed out. 'Wouldn't you have tried to stop them, if you were me?'

'Oh, well,' Orlop muttered. 'I s'pose. But what am *I* gonna do now, without a master?'

Before any of the others could reply, they were interrupted – by a wild shriek of rage. Turning, they saw the princess's sailboat bearing down on them, with her servants glaring at its rails.

'Princess!' shrieked the tall narrow woman furiously. 'Your father the king will hear *all* about this, I promise you! Running away from us like that . . . You may be sure you won't be allowed in *that* boat again, *ever*! And another thing . . .'

She was still shrieking as the sailboat went rushing on past, with the servants again helplessly unable to stop or turn it quickly enough. And Lily looked woefully at Mudjack.

'She's right,' she said. 'My father

probably *will* forbid me to go with you
again, Jack. He's very strict about the
servants being near me all the time.'

Mudjack felt crushed. 'Couldn't they
come along in the sailboat?' he asked.
'If we promised not to leave them
behind?'

'I don't know,' Lily said sighing. 'But it would be so *boring*, having to do everything as slowly as a sailboat. Halyard wouldn't be able to do any of his magical things . . .'

Then she paused, looking puzzled – for Mudjack had begun to grin, his eyes bright with a sudden idea.

'What if your servants had a magic boat of their *own*?' he asked. 'So they could keep up no matter what Hal did?'

'A boat named Orlop!' Halyard said with a laugh.

'Me?' Orlop said, sounding pleased. 'Go into *royal* service? Now wouldn't that be somethin'!'

Lily's eyes were shining. 'Jack, that's wonderful! I'm sure my father would agree!' She looked fondly at Mudjack and Halyard. 'Especially when I tell him what *heroes* you two have been – rescuing my crown, catching that evil pirate . . .'

So they sailed away, with Orlop following, back to the royal pier. From where Lily would take Mudjack to meet her parents, the king and queen. And a message would be sent to Mudjack's parents, to tell them about his amazing new life. And then he and Lily and Halyard would begin their wonderful time of boating up and down the rivers of that land, seeing all the strange and interesting things.

While now and then, whenever they wished, going back to where they had been that day, to see the sea.